THE
GATEWAY

THE
MIDNIGHT
MERCENARY

Cerberus Jones

Kane Miller
A DIVISION OF EDC PUBLISHING

CHAPTER ONE

A bolt of lightning streaked across the sky outside the window, and for a split second Amelia could see the hotel lobby around her. Then, just as quickly, it was utterly dark again, and a thunderclap almost deafened her.

Amelia stood rigid, blinking in the dark, hating the storm, hating the blackout, and knowing there was nothing she could do about either.

"Sonic boom!" Charlie cheered. "That was the closest one yet! I hope –"

He was drowned out as lightning and thunder

1

hit the hotel simultaneously. Amelia felt sick. She also felt something soft rub against her leg, and bent down to scoop up her puppy, Grawk.

It's only a storm, she told herself. But she knew there was nothing *only* about being in a building hit by lightning. A hundred million volts of electricity striking at a temperature of fifty thousand degrees Fahrenheit was the exact opposite of *only*.

Charlie shrieked in excitement. Amelia could hear him jumping around like a lunatic. A lunatic who, for some reason, was singing "Another One Bites the Dust." There was a bang and a sudden yelp of pain.

Another flash of lightning gave Amelia a glimpse of Charlie holding his forehead and standing a bit too close to the corner of the reception desk. She snorted with laughter despite herself, but stopped short at the peal of thunder that rolled over them. The chance of being hit by lightning was only about one in ten thousand, she reminded herself, breathing deeply.

On the other hand, the chance of winning the lottery was less than one in forty-five *million*, and yet people still thought it was worth buying a ticket ...

Charlie groaned. "Did you hear that? A gap

between the lightning and thunder. It's going past already! What a rip-off."

Amelia just shook her head.

A beam of electric light appeared at the end of the corridor, and flashed around the lobby before settling on them both. Amelia's dad had finally found a flashlight in the kitchen.

"Don't worry about missing out on the storm, Charlie," he said, walking over. "This whole headland is so strongly magnetic, it acts like a kind of ... well, *magnet* for electrical storms. There's a good chance this one will circle back to us."

"Awesome!"

Amelia shuddered. "You're mental, Charlie."

Dad put his arm around her. "Don't worry, cookie. We've got lightning rods at every corner of the hotel. We're safe as houses."

"Yeah, I know. It's just a bit ..." She glanced in Charlie's direction. "A bit boring with the

4

blackout."

Dad squeezed her to him. "I'm on it. I found the fuse wire, a flashlight – only one, I'm afraid – and Tom is going to show me where the fuse box is. We'll have the lights back on in no time."

Charlie booed.

"In the meantime," Dad went on, "I've found a box of matches, too. Take them through to your mum and see if they're any better than that dud lighter she's been struggling with."

He shone the flashlight on the matchbox so Amelia could take it, then gave her a kiss and walked out the main doors of the hotel to the pounding rain beyond. The lobby seemed twice as dark as before.

"Come on, Charlie, let's go to the library."

There was no reply.

"Charlie?" She waited. "OK, ha-ha, Charlie, very funny. Where are you?"

But the lobby was silent. Had Charlie slipped out behind Dad? Amelia thought she would have seen him go – an extra shadow, an extra flicker of movement against the thin glow of the flashlight. He might have used the distraction to slink off somewhere else altogether. Amelia had no idea what for, but she'd given up trying to figure out how Charlie's mind worked sometimes.

"All right, then, Grawk," she said. "Just you and me. Library."

The puppy blinked solemnly at her, his molten-gold eyes glowing softly in the darkness. OK, so maybe Grawk wasn't *technically* a puppy – he wasn't any kind of Earth dog at all. He'd appeared a week or so ago in the caves under Tom's cottage – an accidental "blowback" through one of the wormholes that had connected with the gateway. And from the moment Amelia had seen him, had taken him in her arms and felt him snuggle his velvety head under her chin, she'd known he was trusting her to keep him safe.

Charlie still wasn't convinced. They'd met several kinds of aliens since coming to the Gateway Hotel – a tall, fearsome reptile woman, a whole army of tiny pink and purple bearlike warriors, and Leaf Man, who could leap like a grasshopper. But no matter what size or shape they were, whether furry or scaly, all those aliens were undoubtedly *people*. Grawk was the first alien they'd met who seemed to be an animal. Yet Charlie had his suspicions, and whenever Grawk did something even slightly wonderful or extraordinary, he'd narrow his eyes coldly.

Amelia didn't care. It was just jealousy, right?

She bent down to stroke his head. "Can you see in the dark, Grawk?"

He made an odd grinding sound, halfway between a purr and a growl, stood up and turned away from her so that her hand was on the tip of his tail rather than his head. As soon as Amelia held on to his tail, he trotted happily across the lobby to the library, not wavering, not bumping into anything. Amelia stumbled along behind.

In the library doorway she called out, "I've got matches!"

"Thank goodness," said Mum. "Stay where you are, I'll come to – *ow*!"

"I'll come to you," said Amelia, and Grawk led her daintily around the desk, past the old fireplace, between the chairs, and over to the shelf where Mum had lined up all the candles.

It was a huge relief to see some light, and the warm candlelight was a lot more comforting than the gray beam of Dad's flashlight. As Mum lit one candle after another the library began to reappear from the gloom, and Amelia could see James sprawled on a sofa, and Charlie's mum, Mary, fitting yet more candles into holders. One good thing about living in an ancient, spooky hotel that everyone in town said was haunted: they had a lot of candelabra.

"Where's Charlie?" asked Mary.

"I don't know. He disappeared when Dad said he was going to help Tom get the power back on."

Mary made a cross noise. "If he's outside in all this rain ..." she muttered to herself. "If he gives himself pneumonia ... If he thinks he's getting out of school ..."

Amelia had never heard her finish one of these sentences. She wondered if even Mary knew how they should end.

"James," said Mum. "Do you want to take a couple of candelabra and light the lobby for Dad?"

"Not really," said James. He lay back, one arm draped over his eyes, the other dangling to the floor.

Mum's smile tightened. "Let me rephrase that: James, take a couple of candelabra to the lobby."

James sighed and heaved himself off the sofa. He thudded over to the candelabra, took one in each hand, sighed again, and thudded out to the lobby.

Mum and Mary shared a look, and Mum called after him brightly, "Thank you, James!"

Amelia rolled her eyes. She didn't know how her parents could stand it, but she was totally over her brother. He was always moping around. And grumpy. And sarcastic. And not funny, *clever* sarcastic like he used to be. Now he was just mean.

She was still glowering when James came back into the library and slumped onto the sofa as though exhausted by the effort of walking forty feet. He reached over to a shelf beside him and pulled down a book. He was flicking through the opening pages when Lady Naomi stepped through the doorway and looked around at them all. She beamed at Amelia, and Amelia smiled back, her heart lifting. No matter how ferocious the storm outside, if it meant a chance to hang out with Lady Naomi, it was worth it.

Even though Lady Naomi lived at the hotel, and her room was only feet away from Amelia's, they hardly ever saw her. Apart from one memorable evening they had spent with her in the hotel's kitchen, Lady Naomi was always off doing some sort of "research." But what she did or where she did it, Amelia had never found out.

Yet here she was, dressed exactly as she had been the last time Amelia saw her. Her plain black tank top left her arms bare, showing a terrible scar that ran from one shoulder all the way to her wrist. On anyone else, Amelia thought, an injury like that would look disgusting or ugly. Somehow it just made Lady Naomi look even more mysterious and cool.

Lady Naomi walked over to the sofa and sat next to James – so close that James shied away in surprise.

"Hey, watch –" he began, only to choke off when he saw who it was.

"Hi, James," said Lady Naomi. Her voice was husky, and a little bit breathy. Like she'd been running up and down the stairs. Not that Amelia could imagine Lady Naomi getting winded.

Grawk pricked up his ears and stared at her.

"Um. Uh ..." James coughed. "Hello."

Even by candlelight, Amelia could see he was blushing. James had been obsessed with Lady Naomi since before he'd even *met* her, but this was the first time she'd shown any particular interest in him.

Lady Naomi smiled at James – a wide, wicked smile that crinkled her nose. "James, I was thinking ..." she said, and leaned over to him. She was much shorter than James, and had to reach up to whisper in his ear. "Tomorrow, after this storm passes, maybe you and I could ..."

Amelia's mouth dropped open. She couldn't make out what Lady Naomi was saying now, but as she watched, the stunned look on James's face gradually shifted to wonder, to a dawning, impossible happiness, and then –

Lady Naomi gave a great snort and began laughing helplessly, slapping her knee in a way that caught Mary's attention immediately.

"Is that *you*, Charlie?" his mum called hesitantly. Then, "Karolos Floros!" followed by a torrent of angry Greek.

On the sofa, Lady Naomi reached up to her neck. A moment later, her whole body flickered and disappeared, and Amelia saw Charlie sitting in her place, a small brass object clutched between his fingers.

It was a holo-emitter – one of the devices Tom used to disguise all the alien guests who stayed at the hotel.

So he's finally worked out how to use it, Amelia thought. *Great.*

"Oh, Charlie," said Mum sadly, but she was looking at James.

James stood up, his face red again, but this time with fury. Charlie was still laughing to himself, ignoring his mum and apparently quite unaware that James was about to go volcanic.

Amelia had never seen James so mad. He drew back his fist as though he were about to punch Charlie, but – though Charlie almost deserved it – he lowered it again and yelled instead.

"You pathetic, thieving scumbag! You went into my room? You went through my things? You stole that –" He broke off, making a grab for the holo-emitter.

Charlie twisted away, but he finally stopped laughing and looked up at James. It seemed to take a second or two for him to work out just how mad James really was. Amelia watched Charlie's face slide from confusion, to surprise, to a certain wide-eyed realization that clearly said *uh-oh* ...

But rather than yelling at Charlie again, James turned instead on Mum. "You see?" he bellowed. "You dragged me out here, away from all my friends, away from everything good for *this?*" He pointed at Charlie in disgust.

Mum was silent.

Amelia ground her teeth. James was doing the same thing he'd been doing ever since they'd first arrived here: getting angry as an excuse for ignoring the facts. Nearly a month in the hotel, a month surrounded by alien technology and alien wormholes – not to mention the aliens themselves – and James had spent the whole time trying desperately to convince himself that none of it was actually happening. Bizarrely, he'd even spent a few days tinkering with this holo-emitter as a way of distracting himself from reality.

And now he was doing the same thing all over again, concentrating as hard as he could on the one thing he could deal with (they had moved) to avoid facing the truth: that he had just seen genuine alien technology at work.

Charlie, meanwhile, was sitting frozen, as though hoping that if he stayed still enough, James would forget he was there. Amelia didn't know who to feel sorrier for. On the other hand, it was also hard to tell who was being the bigger jerk.

But before things had the chance to escalate any further, a flash of lightning lit up the room, making their candles seem pale for an instant, and Amelia saw the face of a grizzled old man through the glass of the library's French doors. He was streaming with water, his gray hair flat to his head, and his black eye patch stark against his skin. As the thunder boomed, he knocked three times using a hand that was missing a finger. He looked like the ghost of a drowned sailor.

Mary spun around with a little squeal of surprise.

"Oh, for goodness sake," said Mum. "Tom!"

CHAPTER TWO

"Quickly, Amelia," said Mum. "Let Tom in."

Charlie, who was quick to recognize a good distraction when he saw one, had leapt off the sofa and was already halfway to the doors. Tom, although under the shelter of the hotel's veranda, was standing in the middle of his own personal puddle. Water dribbled off his trousers.

"Come in, Tom," said Mum. "Dry off before you catch your death."

Tom twitched at the words, although Amelia knew they only meant that Tom shouldn't risk a cold. "No time," he said gruffly. He went to keep talking but stopped and frowned at Charlie beside him, and then at Amelia.

"Can you get the power back on?" Mum asked. "Scott's usually faster than this with a fuse box."

Tom rubbed his nose with the back of his hand and didn't answer.

"Well?" Mum prompted.

Tom glanced at Charlie and Amelia again, and raised a helpless eyebrow at Mum.

"I'm sorry," she said briskly. "You came here to tell us something, not to be pestered with questions. What was it you needed?"

"We've got guests coming," said Tom.

A shiver sparked up Amelia's back. If Tom knew about the guests first, that meant they were aliens, traveling through a wormhole in space and arriving at the gateway in the caves under his cottage.

Mum sighed. "How many of them?"

"And how long until they arrive?" Mary added.

According to hotel rules, off-world guests were supposed to send Tom a message at least a day or two in advance, to give Dad time to sort out the strange foods some aliens needed, and Mum and Mary time to sort out any special arrangements for the rooms.

"An hour or two," said Tom apologetically.

"*What?*" said Mum.

"And there will be about twenty of them."

"*How* many?" said Mary.

"Mostly children," said Tom. "Sorry."

"In a blackout!" Mum almost yelled. "Trekking through the rain and mud in the middle of the night, and we can't offer them so much as a cup of hot tea, let alone a bath!"

Lightning flashed into the room, but no thunder followed. Amelia looked at Charlie, who quickly put his hands behind his back.

"Yeah ..." Tom looked awkward. "It was a bit of a last-minute thing ..."

"How can moving twenty-odd children across space be a last-minute thing?" Mum really was yelling now. "Why on earth would anyone leave plans like that until the last –" She caught herself, realized something, and shook off her temper. "Right. Sorry, Tom," she said calmly. "I just had a tiny little mental overload there for a second. I'm back now. So, what do you need us to do?"

"I'm afraid I don't know," he said warily. "There were no other details given."

"Right," said Mum. "Very good. Thank you, Tom."

As Tom turned to go, Amelia saw Charlie slip out into the lobby.

Not so fast, Charlie, thought Amelia. He might be able to sneak off on the two mums, and

21

maybe even outrun James for a while, but Amelia wouldn't let him go so easily.

The lobby was eerie in the half dark. The candelabra that James had left lit up the reception desk well enough, but that only made the rest of the room feel darker, more echoing. Amelia looked instinctively towards the twin staircases, as though she might be able to see Charlie there, if only she looked hard enough. Her eyes ached with the darkness. She'd never realized how tiring it was to *not* see.

Behind her, she heard the main doors to the hotel creak open, and the sound of the rain grew louder. Charlie was going *out?*

Grawk made that rumbling sound again, and Amelia followed the faint glow of his eyes towards the door. Standing on the threshold, not sure whether to go out into the night, she heard a voice call, "Tom! Tom!"

Amelia gasped. It was her *mother*.

"Yes?" Tom called back, and Amelia heard his boots coming closer along the wooden veranda. "What is it, Skye?"

"Just one thing," Mum said. "You didn't want to say anything about the power. Why? What's wrong?"

Tom sucked in his breath, and for a long pause there was nothing but the sound of the rain. Amelia strained her ears as much as her eyes.

"Skye, I don't know how to say this, but ..."

"What?"

"I couldn't say anything in front of the kids ..."

"*What?*"

"It's everything we feared, Skye."

This time Mum's voice was shaky. "What?"

"Keep the kids inside. Don't let them out of your sight for a moment."

"Why?" Mum sounded like a kid herself.

"Another wormhole connected this evening, a couple of hours ago, and someone came through. It was –" Tom faltered. "Well, I've just received confirmation – it was Krskn."

Amelia felt her heart lurch. She knew Krskn only by name – but every time she'd ever heard that name spoken, it was in anxious, fearful tones. Whenever anyone talked about danger coming through the gateway, whenever they talked about absolute, terrifying worst-case scenarios,

Krskn was the name that came up.

"He's *here?*" Mum said.

"And he's cut the power," said Tom. "Whatever he's here for, he wants us in the dark."

"OK," said Mum, trying to rally. "OK. It's Krskn, and he's cut the power. OK. We can deal with that."

"I'm sorry, Skye. But that's not all."

Amelia bit her lip so hard she tasted blood. Even more frightening than the thought of Krskn out there messing with them was the sorrow in Tom's voice. And then he said it:

"I'm sorry, Skye. He's already got Scott."

CHAPTER THREE

Amelia ran out of the hotel and immediately collided with someone. She felt Mum's hands catch her. "Where is he?" she yelled to Tom. "Where's my dad?"

"Get her inside, Skye!" Tom bellowed. "Now!"

Amelia shoved at Mum, pushing against her in anger as she was dragged back into the lobby, leaving Tom outside. Mum's body flickered, disappeared and suddenly it was *Charlie* grabbing her fists and saying, "Shh! Stop it, Amelia, it's me!"

"I know it's you, you creep!" she hissed, grasping

for the holo-emitter. "How could you do that? Give it to me! I'm going to smash it –"

"What's going on?" This time it really was her mum, silhouetted in the library doorway. "Amelia! What's happened?"

"Dad's gone!" Amelia cried.

"What? Gone where?" She hurried over to Amelia.

"Krskn took him! I don't know where."

Mum staggered slightly, but her voice was steady. "Krskn? Why do you think that?"

"Tom said!" Amelia shouted, and then added viciously, "Ask Charlie – he's the one Tom told."

"Charlie?" his mum asked, confused but already suspicious. "Why would Tom –?"

"It doesn't matter why," Charlie said quickly. "Tom told us – told me," he admitted, "that Krskn was here, that he cut the power, and he took Mr. Walker."

Mum was silent for several long seconds. In the dim candlelight of the lobby, Amelia could see her pale face frowning in concentration. Then her shoulders squared and she lifted her chin.

"So," said Mum. "Here's the situation: in an hour or so, more than twenty aliens, mostly children, will arrive at the hotel. For whatever reason, they gave us no real warning that they were coming. Now we have Krskn somewhere loose on the grounds, cutting our power and leaving us blind – I don't think it's too big a leap of logic to assume he's targeting the kids."

"Us?" Charlie gasped.

"No, not you – the alien kids. Which means two things: one, these children need our protection. We must do everything we can to keep them safe."

"Right," said Amelia shakily.

"And two," said Mum, "doing so is going to put us all in mortal danger."

Mum led them back into the library. James was still lounging on the sofa, a little pile of books now gathering on the floor beside him.

"All right, sis?" he asked lazily. "Did you see a ghost?"

"That's enough, James," Mum snapped. "We're in real trouble right now, and whether you like it or not, you're involved."

"Me?" James was indignant. "What did I do?"

"It's not about you, James!" Amelia yelled. "It's about Dad!"

"What happened to Dad?"

"He's been kidnapped," said Mum, utterly matter-of-fact.

"He's *what?* Kidnapped? Oh, come on now –"

Mum ignored him and went on. "The kidnapper's still out there, which means there's hope of finding your dad. But it *also* means that any one of us could be next. All of you need to stay inside the hotel. At all times. Preferably in the library itself, do you understand?"

Amelia nodded, feeling cold.

"Stay where you've got light, and stick together so you can watch out for each other. Mary, go and get the first aid kit. With so many young guests coming, we should have it near. And when they do arrive, bring them in here, too. I assume they already understand the situation, and they won't mind bunkering down in here for the night."

Mary nodded and rushed out of the room. But Amelia saw a problem. "Why are you telling Mary what to do? Why can't you do it?"

Mum smiled sadly and Amelia knew what she was about to say. "Because I'm going out to find Dad and help Tom."

"No!" Amelia was close to panic. "Not you, too!

You have to stay here with us."

"Cookie." Mum hugged her. "Don't you want me to help Dad?"

"Yes, but –"

"It's OK, Amelia. I know how to do this. Diplomatic work isn't all sitting at a desk and going to balls, you know. I've done some ... fieldwork in my time. And Gateway Control have made sure I've got some tools for the job."

"You mean a gun?" asked Charlie.

Mum smiled. "Not a gun."

"You'd be better off with a gun," said Amelia.

"A gun?" James scoffed. "What is this, one of those role-playing games? Because I get it now – so, like, Dad's Professor Mustard in the library, and we've got to solve the crime, right?"

Amelia gritted her teeth. "*We're* in the library, James. And Dad's *missing*. What part of that seems like a game to you?"

"The part where Mum gets a gun and runs off into the night like James Bond."

Mum turned to him, took his face in both hands, and kissed him on the forehead. "I love you, James. Stay in the library and promise me you'll try not to get yourself kidnapped before you figure out which one of us here is playing games with himself."

James's mouth dropped open, but he quickly shut it and put on his usual sneer.

Mum hugged Amelia tightly. "Be safe, sweetheart. I'll be back soon, and with Dad, OK?"

Amelia nodded, not able to speak, and then Mum was gone – out of the library, and out of the hotel, into the same darkness that was hiding Krskn.

What if Mum never came back? What if that was the last time Amelia ever saw her? That could have been literally the last second Amelia had parents. For all she knew, she was already an orphan.

Charlie patted her on the back. "At least it's stopped raining," he said kindly. "Your mum won't get too wet."

Amelia knew Charlie was trying to make up for his stupid stunts with the holo-emitter, but it was too much for her right now. She was too frightened, and still too angry. Tricking James had been slack and stupid, but pretending to be her mum was just wrong. He'd used Mum's voice to get information out of Tom, and that had been using Tom, too.

Charlie hadn't meant any harm, she knew that. He never did, but that didn't make his stunts any better. She didn't even want to *look* at him right now. Instead, she settled down on the floor and played with Grawk. She made a fist, and Grawk curled himself into a ball, wrapping his tail tightly around his paws and flatting back his ears. Then she opened her hand out like a star, and he leapt into the air with his legs stretched wide and his mouth split into a grin. He landed silently.

Amelia put two fingers on the ground and walked them around. Grawk stood up on his back paws and toddled a dozen or so steps towards her.

"How do you make him do that?" Charlie marveled. Amelia rolled her eyes. Like Charlie was actually suddenly interested in Grawk.

"He's amazing," Charlie went on. "You can make him do anything!"

"I don't make him. I just sort of ... suggest things, and see if he agrees."

Charlie regarded the creature with cautious respect. Grawk was still standing awkwardly when he suddenly dropped to all fours, spun away from Amelia and raced to the library's French doors.

"Grawk?" Amelia scrambled to her feet.

He flicked one ear back to show he'd heard her, but he didn't turn from whatever it was he'd seen out there.

"Grawk?" she said again, the hair prickling on the back of her neck. Was something out there in the dark? It could be Mum. Or Tom. But the way Grawk was behaving ...

He barked sharply. Not once, but over and over.

"Shut it, dog," said James, throwing a shoe at him.

Grawk kept barking.

"Amelia, shut your dog up, will you?"

Mary stopped and peered at him anxiously. "I've never heard him bark before."

"What do you think he means, Amelia?" said Charlie.

James snorted. "What does it *mean?* What is it *saying?* It's not Lassie, guys – there is no special message. It's a *dog*. If it's saying anything at all, it's, 'Let me out, I'm busting for a pee.'"

Without waiting for a response, he got off the sofa, pushed past Charlie and Amelia, and opened the French doors. Grawk stopped barking and sped out into the night. Being entirely black, he disappeared almost instantly.

"You ... you ... *moron!*" Amelia screeched. "Why did you do that?"

And to her total embarrassment, she burst into tears.

"Oh, grow up, Amelia," said James. "Not everyone around here wants to keep indulging you in your stupid make-believe. It's about time you started living in the real –"

But Amelia had had more than enough of James's stupidity. She'd already lost two parents tonight – she wasn't about to lose Grawk as well. Without another thought, Amelia ran through the open door and into the dark.

CHAPTER FOUR

"Amelia, wait!" Charlie yelled from close behind. He must have run into the garden after her.

"Go back!" she shouted. "I don't want you to get caught too!"

"Too late," said Charlie, zeroing in on the sound of her voice. "Anyway, I owe you."

"For what?" Amelia was impatient, but couldn't deny it felt better to have Charlie out here with her.

"For being kind of a massive suck-head before. You know, with the holo-emitter and stuff."

"And *stuff*," Amelia repeated. "That covers a lot."

"Yeah."

There was a silence, and then Charlie said, "Well?"

"Well what?"

"Do you forgive me? Can we get on with being friends, or what?"

Amelia laughed bitterly. "That was an *apology?*"

Charlie sighed. "Look, Amelia, I'm only going to say this once, and I'm only saying it at all because we're totally in the dark and I can't see you and we're probably both going to die any minute anyway, but –" He drew in a deep breath. "The fact is, you're my best friend, and you would be even if I had other friends. Your family is practically the only good thing that has happened to me since I was three years old and my dad took me to Uluru, and I never, ever want to do anything to make any of you hate me and not want me around. Ever."

Amelia felt very quiet. "Oh."

"Right," said Charlie. "So can we get a move on and find Grawk before Krskn catches us?"

That was a terrific idea, but Amelia hadn't a clue where to start. Now that the rain had stopped, the clouds were thinning and there was the slightest haze of moonlight in the air. It wasn't nearly enough to see by, but Amelia could just make out the rough shape of the grounds around her. She looked back at the hotel, at the light gleaming through the library's French doors, and tried to figure out the rough direction Grawk had been staring in before James let him out. Amelia turned to get her bearings.

"This way," she said.

They bumped along through the sodden grass, and Amelia stumbled on the edge of a flower bed.

"Are you OK?" Charlie whispered.

"Yes," she whispered back, wondering if Krskn were sitting in the bushes beside them right that very moment. How did he do it? The kidnapping or murdering or whatever it was he did? Would he hit them over the head and shove them into a bag, or did he have spring-loaded traps hidden under leaves? Or perhaps he had a ray gun and would freeze them before they even knew he was there. She hoped it was the ray gun.

"Where to now?" asked Charlie.

Amelia hesitated. Ahead of them and off a bit to one side, she saw something. It was faintly yellow, and coming closer. She clutched Charlie's arm. "Look!"

It was Grawk, silent and nearly invisible except for those luminous eyes.

Amelia bent down to him. "Where did you go?" She scratched behind his ears. "I was so worried. Well, come on. We're going to get in huge trouble with Charlie's mum because of you."

But Grawk had other ideas. Standing on his

41

back legs, he delicately nipped her fingers and pulled her forward – away from the hotel.

"What's going on?" Charlie hissed.

"I think … he wants us to follow him."

Charlie grunted. "He'd better be on our side. I'll feel pretty stupid if he just invited us to go and meet his old pal, Krskn."

But Amelia trusted Grawk fully. She bent over to hold his tail, and took Charlie's hand. They followed the alien dog in an awkward line through the dark. He took them around the edge of the rose gardens, down a side path to the back of the hotel, and through some very closely grown, scratchy bushes. Just as Amelia started to wonder if he was chasing random smells in the grass, he stopped. The moon had come out enough now for her to see they were standing in front of a small brick building with a wooden door.

"Go on," Charlie whispered.

She pulled the door open, wincing as the hinges squealed, shockingly loud in the night. To her surprise, Dad's flashlight was lying on the floor in front of her, its electric beam starting to fade and pointing uselessly at the wall.

Coming from inside the room, she heard a scuffle – feet scraping on dusty concrete and kicking at bricks. Without thinking, she snatched the flashlight and shone it into the room. If they were about to be attacked by Krskn, at least they would see him coming.

The beam flashed over a wall of different dials and meters, as well as a ruined fuse box, but what grabbed Amelia's attention were the *legs* in the far corner of the room. Dad's legs. His feet were tapping the ground to make sure she found him – but where was Dad's *body?* Above his waist was nothing but blackness and shadows.

For one horrifying second, Amelia thought her

father had been sliced in half, and Krskn had left only the legs behind, somehow still nightmarishly alive. But then she realized that Dad's body had been glued to the wall by an enormous band of what looked like tar. It bound his arms to his sides and pressed him hard into the corner, holding him flat against the bricks, and covering him right up to his nose. He could still breathe, hear and see, but apart from tapping his feet he was helpless.

"Dad!" Amelia cried, and started towards him, but before she could touch him, he kicked the wall violently and glared.

Amelia stopped short and stared at him, confused. He started tapping on the floor again. "Dad?"

He kept tapping.

"He's doing Morse code!" said Charlie. "The tapping!"

Now Amelia listened carefully, and she could hear the repeating rhythm too. "What's he saying?"

"GO," said Charlie. "Just: GO, GO, GO."

"No." Amelia looked at Dad. "Grawk brought us here to save you. We're not leaving you."

Her dad tapped again, slowly and clearly so Charlie could follow. "GO ... NOW... KRSKN ... HERE ... DANGER ... no, wait, DANGER*OUS* ... FOR ... YOU."

"I don't care," said Amelia.

Dad tapped.

"What?" said Amelia, as Charlie paused and grimaced.

"PLEASE, COOKIE."

Amelia couldn't move. She had found her dad – how could she just walk away and leave him to Krskn? It wasn't possible.

She was still standing there, wondering what to do, when she heard branches snapping outside and the heavy thud of boots. She lurched around, the flashlight flashing over Charlie's horrified face before dazzling the burly figure pushing through the bushes to reach them.

"Put that down," the figure said gruffly. "Want to blind me?"

"Tom?" Amelia dropped the light from Tom's face and waited for her heart to restart in her chest. Grawk, she noticed, was sitting calmly beside her. Obviously Tom hadn't taken *him* by surprise.

"What are you two doing out of the hotel?" Tom hissed. "I know you heard me, Amelia – Krskn's *here* somewhere."

"And now I know where my dad is!" she hissed back.

"So what? You can't undo the binding tar, so you're no use to your dad. All you're doing is handing yourselves to Krskn for free, and what good is that going to do anyone?"

Brutal as ever. Amelia couldn't argue with Tom, though. As usual he was right, but she refused to leave just yet. She turned to Dad. "Does it hurt?"

He tapped.

"NO," said Charlie. "NOT ... AT ... ALL." And then, as Dad kept tapping, he went on, "BUT ... I ... HAVE ... A ... TERRIBLE ... ITCH ... ON ... MY ... NOSE."

Amelia tried to smile as she stepped forward to scratch the end of Dad's long nose. It was hardly a hug or a kiss or even a real good-bye, but it was all she could do right now.

He tapped again.

"GO," said Charlie. "GO ... NOW. QUICKLY."

"Come on," said Tom. "This door made enough noise to wake the dead when you opened it. It got my attention anyway, and I was halfway down the hill. It's almost certain Krskn knows we're all here."

That got Amelia moving. She didn't feel any better about leaving Dad, but she couldn't stand it if Charlie was kidnapped because of her. She set the flashlight on the floor so that it pointed at the roof, lighting up the whole meter room with an electric glow that was getting fainter by the minute, but was hopefully better than nothing.

She followed Charlie and Tom back into the grounds. The moon was still trying to shine through the clouds, but thunder was starting to rumble again in the distance. Every now and then a cloud flicked on like a giant lamp as lightning sparked inside it.

Amelia trudged through the grass, utterly defeated. How stupid not to be able to do anything. How ghastly if all they could do was sit back and let Krskn do whatever he wanted.

"Isn't there something we can do?" Charlie asked.

"You?" Tom said. "No. But –"

"What about my mum?" Amelia interrupted.

"What about her?"

"Whatever she's doing – is it helping?"

Tom wheeled around to face them both. "Skye's out here? Alone?"

"She came out here to help *you*!"

He made an angry grunt. "I thought she was the only one of you with a bit of sense. Come on." He turned back and kept walking, muttering something about fish in a barrel.

Just as they reached the main steps to the hotel, Grawk gave a low growl.

"What is it?" Amelia bent to stroke him, and felt that all the fur on his back was bristling. "Grawk?"

Without another sound, he shot off down the hill and disappeared. Amelia would have called out to him, but Tom had already wrapped a hand over her mouth.

"Come on – *now*," he hissed furiously. And taking them each by an arm, he dragged Amelia and Charlie up to the library's doors and knocked on the glass.

Mary was there in a second, the heavy poker from the fireplace in one hand and a desperate look on her face. She unlatched the door and when Tom shoved Amelia and Charlie through the gap, she broke into tears. "Where have you *been?* You could have been killed!" she sobbed, hugging Charlie, shaking him hard, and hugging him again. "And you," she said, pulling Amelia into the huddle.

"If they step foot outside this hotel again, I'll kill them myself," said Tom. "You got that?"

Amelia nodded, too overwhelmed to speak.

"Tom, what on earth is going on?" said Mary. "What is all this *about?*"

Tom snorted. "Do you want the good news, or

the bad?"

"Both! Just tell me the truth."

"The good news is, I've heard that Krskn isn't here to murder, torture or get revenge on anyone."

Mary nodded, waiting for him to go on.

"The bad news," Tom went on, "is that he's here to kidnap as many of our guests as he can. And he'll do whatever it takes to get the job done – *including* murder and torture, if anyone gets in his way."

Amelia heard this and was numb. Between shock and grief for her dad, fear for her mum, and the loss of Grawk a second time, Tom's news was too much to absorb. She looked over at the sofa. There was James, a book still in his hand, not paying attention to anything that was happening. Anger flared inside her.

It must be nice to be a total brain-dead jerk, she thought. *Very relaxing.*

CHAPTER FIVE

While James sat in the corner and read, Tom gave Amelia, Charlie and his mum the first sliver of hope they'd had all night.

"Now, as I was *trying* to tell you," he said gruffly, "someone's coming. If we can just hold out a bit longer, we won't be on our own with Krskn."

"Control is sending an agent?" asked Charlie.

"Those bureaucrats!" spat Tom. "No. We're waiting for someone with actual power."

"Who?"

"A Keeper," Tom said impressively.

There was a pause, and Charlie said, "A what?"

"A Keeper of the Gates and Ways," said Tom, emphasizing the importance of each word.

Amelia and Charlie swapped a look. *OK* ...

"And this – this gatekeeper person," said Mary. "You're saying they're a match for Krskn?"

Tom looked as though he'd like to correct her phrasing – but then suddenly, from outside, came the sound of boots and voices – lots of both, and no one trying to be quiet.

"The guests!" said Mary. "I almost forgot them in all this chaos," and she dashed out to the lobby to open the main doors.

Amelia followed, carrying with her another candelabra in each hand to bring a bit more light to the gloomy entrance.

There, tramping through the doors with mud smearing the floor behind them, wet and shivering under their backpacks, was a troop of

Scouts about Amelia and Charlie's age. A couple of worried-looking adults waved them through, counting heads. So *many* heads that Amelia found herself joining in – past twenty, past thirty until they stopped at forty-five Scouts. Another three adult leaders brought up the rear.

Mary was astonished. "But we only had a reservation for twenty-two!"

Two of the Scout leaders took off their packs with great groans of relief, and glanced at each other. "Yes, sorry about this ..." the older one began. "A bit of a disaster, really ..."

But before he could go on, a third Scout leader stepped over and clapped him heartily on the back. "Nonsense! We all made it here, didn't we? Just a bit more adventure than we expected, isn't it?"

"You can say that again ..." the older leader muttered.

"What's going on?" Mary asked faintly.

The cheerful Scout leader reached over and shook her hand with both of his. He smiled gratefully and as he moved into the candlelight, Amelia saw that he was extremely handsome.

"Hello, I'm Derek," he said. "It's so good of you to take us on such short notice. Or, as it turns out for half of us, with no notice at all!"

Mary laughed nervously, one hand still in Derek's, the other stealing up to touch her throat. "Half of you?" she echoed weakly.

"It was the strangest thing." Derek's eyes twinkled as he smiled. "You couldn't make this stuff up. There we were, our campsite flooded, and no option but to take off through the bush and look for shelter. No idea where we were going – the maps were ruined, and our compasses went haywire."

That crazy magnetism under the headland, thought Amelia.

"We were completely lost," Derek continued,

"and then – what happens? We bump into another mob of Scouts in exactly the same predicament! Incredible!"

"Two groups of Scouts?" Mary said, and Amelia knew what she was thinking. Had the alien guests from the gateway bumped into a troop of real human Scouts on their way up the hill and decided to copy the uniforms with their holo-emitters?

Or – and this would make things triply complicated – had two groups of human Scouts really been out camping at the same time, and just decided to make for the nearest shelter? In that case, there would still be aliens on the way, and they could end up with over *seventy* guests for the night. All in the one library ...

She looked at Tom for a clue, but he was gazing at the Scouts in amazement. "I don't know," he said when Mary raised her eyebrows at him. "They're a bit early, but ..."

Amelia knew what he was unable to say in front of visitors: the wormholes had been increasingly unpredictable lately, and it was harder and harder for Tom to match up his old timetables with the actual arrivals at the gateway. He hadn't expected the aliens to arrive yet, but they *could* have ...

"I'd, uh, better go and check," he said, and limped out into the dark.

Amelia wondered how Charlie's mum was going to deal with all this, but before Mary could even open her mouth, Derek was solving problems for her.

"Look, I'm sorry to inconvenience you like this, but I promise we can take care of ourselves. We've got dry clothes in our packs, and can bunk down anywhere you'd like to put us, uh ..." He paused, and then smiled in embarrassment. "I'm sorry, I don't even know your name."

"Mary," she said, sounding strangled, and

reached up to tuck her hair behind her ear. It was rather girlish and Charlie gave her a sharp look.

"Mary," Derek repeated. "We're at your mercy. Point the way."

James was not at all happy to have fifty wet, smelly Scouts march into his quiet library. He was even less impressed when about half of them immediately started pulling off their muddy boots, peeling off filthy socks and waggling their wrinkly, blistered toes around. They rummaged through their packs for something dry to wear, but then one of the boys caught sight of Amelia, and froze.

"It's all right," said Amelia. "There's a little annex through here – look." She slid open a panel door to reveal a narrow room with bookshelves along one wall and a row of framed pictures on the other. "You can take turns."

There was a great deal of jostling and noise

as the Scouts organized themselves into warm clothes. Although, not all of them. Amelia noticed that half of them seemed content in their wet gear. She nudged Charlie, who nodded. She was pretty sure the aliens were here. Either they only *looked* wet, and were perfectly dry and comfortable under their holo-emitter disguises, or they were the kind of aliens who didn't mind being cold and soggy.

Mary had bustled James off to get towels from the upstairs linen closet (she wasn't letting Charlie or Amelia out of the library again), and had brought out a massive plastic container of Dad's homemade cookies. Soon the Scouts had pushed back the chairs and table, made space on the floor, and were sitting in a wobbly circle, passing the cookie box from hand to hand.

Dad's cookies were a bit of a gamble. Some were perfectly normal chocolate chip cookies, using a perfectly normal recipe. Others had been tweaked a bit – like adding crushed mint candy canes to the double-chocolate brownies. And some were straight out mad-scientist experiments, like the ones made with Vegemite, raisins and curry powder. As the cookies went around the group, it turned into a game of cookie roulette – in the candlelight, no one really knew what they were picking. Each time a Scout took a cookie, everyone held their breath, waiting for the reaction to the first bite.

Sometimes, the Scouts would chew a few times, then smile and say, "Custard and strawberry jelly," and the rest of the group would sigh in disappointment. Then around the box would go: coconut lemon bar, butterscotch shortbread, gingersnaps, and then just as everyone was getting a bit bored, the next Scout would splutter and gag and gasp, "I don't even know – pickle and apricot jam?"

The room would erupt in a roar of delight, and around the box would go again.

Charlie was down there with them, grinning broadly as the girl next to him spat a mouthful of cookie into her hands and shuddered. Amelia, though, sat back from the group and only watched. She was glad the Scouts – humans and aliens alike – were having a good time, but she'd had too much stress tonight to shrug it off and play. The behavior of the Scout leaders wasn't helping her relax, either.

Two of them, Kev and Lorraine – she guessed they were probably the humans – were trying to figure out how far back in the bush their abandoned campsite was, and how long it would take them tomorrow to trek back to recover their equipment. Two others, Barry and Terry, were almost silent. They nodded or grunted in agreement or sympathy every now and then when Kev or Lorraine tried to include them in the conversation, but mostly they just stared at the kids with bleak, exhausted eyes. Only Derek showed any interest in the kids' game.

As Amelia watched, he slid off his chair and squashed into the circle to take his turn at the cookie box. He smiled and laughed along with the kids, and when the box reached him, every kid was wide-eyed, waiting to see what he chose. He bit into his cookie with a grand flourish.

"Mmf, my favorite!" he mumbled through his full mouth.

All the kids groaned.

"Toenails and pill bug!" Derek went on. "Crunchy and nutritious!"

The kids all screamed in disgust.

Despite herself, Amelia smiled. *That* was what a real leader should be like – helping everyone relax and have fun. Sitting around at a separate table, complaining or silently freaking out wasn't helping anyone.

As if he felt her looking at him, Derek turned and smiled at Amelia.

"Are you going to have a turn?" he asked, taking a cookie out of the box and offering it to her.

She shook her head and blushed slightly.

"Ah, very sensible of you." He passed the cookie to the Scout sitting next to him instead. "You can never be too careful, can you?"

Even as he said so, the Scout next to him dropped the cookie to the floor and gasped. Everyone howled with laughter.

"What was it, Len?" a boy shouted over the din. "Mustard and rhubarb?"

The boy had his back to Amelia, but across the other side of the circle, she saw another Scout's face drop with shock.

"Look!" She pointed. "He's choking!"

Horribly, it took her three or four tries to get anyone to listen, and by the time the rest of the Scouts realized there was a problem, Len had collapsed sideways onto the floor and was shaking all over. Derek crouched over him, his eyes wide.

"Len!" Terry yelled from the leader's table. "What happened?"

"Oh, my word!" Lorraine leapt to her feet. "He's frothing at the mouth!"

"It's an allergic reaction," said Derek calmly. "He ate a peanut butter cookie."

James, for the first time all night, threw aside his book and came to see what was wrong.

"He needs a shot," he said. "He can't breathe – look! Where's his medicine?"

"Medicine?" said Barry. "He doesn't have any –"

"I'll get the first aid kit!" James rushed to the

other side of the room.

"But he's not –" Barry and Terry looked at one another in panic. "Len needs –"

"I know what he needs." Derek eyed them both steadily. His face was a remarkable combination of authority and confidence. "I know exactly how to keep him safe. How to keep him healthy."

It seemed to Amelia that Derek had said that awkwardly – he was putting all the importance on the word *keep*, instead of on *safe* and *healthy*.

He said, "You look after the others. I'll *keep* Len with me."

There it was again, and this time, Barry and Terry blinked in wonder and just nodded obediently.

Keep, Amelia thought. *Tom said something about a Keeper. Could Derek be ...?*

She gazed at him, and perhaps he guessed what she was thinking, because just as James rushed up with the red first aid bag, Derek said to her, "It's water Len needs. Can you get me a bucketful? As much as you can carry."

"I can do that," said Charlie, grabbing another candle and pelting out of the room.

By now James had unzipped the bag and was rifling through bandages and swabs looking for the emergency shot of adrenaline, but Derek interrupted him.

"We need to move him *now*."

James shook his head. "What? No! As if we have time to –"

"*Now*," Derek repeated. "Without delay. Into the annex."

Amelia was disturbed. Was Derek really going to make Len wait for his shot while they moved him to another place? It didn't make any sense, but arguing would only slow them down further, so she ran to the annex door and slid it open.

Derek and James carried Len inside.

In the pale light of the candelabra, they laid the limp Scout on the floor. Thick green mucus was bubbling out of Len's mouth. He was on one side and lay utterly still, with no sign that he was breathing.

"You're crazy!" James fell back and stared at Derek. "I think he just died and *you* wasted his last seconds. You killed him!"

In that moment, Charlie staggered in with a bucket slopping water over the edges. Derek nodded in satisfaction.

"Close the door, please," he said to Amelia. Taking the bucket from Charlie, he poured the water over Len's head. He nudged Len with his foot so Len rolled onto his back, and Derek made sure the rest of the water fell onto Len's face and into his open mouth.

"And now you're *drowning* him?" James gasped.

But rather than drowning, Len's whole body jolted. He twitched, writhed on the floor in apparent agony, and then sneezed so violently a wad of green froth spattered the floor and wall.

Almost instantly, there was a hard bang against the wall behind them. Turning, Amelia saw her brother had stumbled backward, hitting his head and shoulder. His face was white with terror; he was staring fascinated and horrified at Len.

To be fair, Len was quite a surprise for anyone.

The sneeze had dislodged his holo-emitter, which now lay sparking on the annex floor. Len himself, uncloaked from his holographic disguise, was now unmistakably *alien* – a giant slug, translucent and glistening, with a mouth wide enough to engulf James's whole head. Two green hearts could be seen beating deep inside his body, while his digestive system made an oddly beautiful squiggly line through his middle, shading from

purple to blue to black. His antennae were retracted miserably into his head, and he trembled as yet more green mucus foamed out of his mouth.

"It wasn't a peanut allergy at all, was it?" said Amelia. "It was the *salt* in the peanut butter that made him sick. Just like an Earth slug."

"Correct," said Derek grimly. "You're a clever kid ..." He paused.

"Amelia."

"Amelia," he nodded. "Well, Len should be OK in a couple of hours. He just needs rest to get over the trauma, and he'll need to stay here, now that his holo-emitter is broken."

Len didn't say anything. He just shuddered.

There was a soft choking noise, but it wasn't Len. Amelia gazed at James coolly.

"What's wrong with him?" said Charlie. "Does he have a salt allergy too? I can get another bucket of water."

"H-how ...?" James stammered. "W-what ...?"

"That's right, James," said Amelia. "He's an alien."

"A Lellum," Derek added. "One of the few to escape his dying home world. This little group tonight are almost all that is left of the whole Lellum race."

James struggled to his feet, disgust twisting his face. "But that's not ... you can't ... I won't ..." He clapped both hands over his mouth and stared again. He looked at Len's gelatinous gray body, the trails of silver slime that sparkled in the candlelight where Len had thrashed around, and the undeniably freaky sight of one of Len's eyeballs telescoping out of his head on its antenna and swiveling around to look at James.

James ducked his head, swallowed, then looked back again at Len. "It's all true, isn't it?" he moaned. "Every bit of it. It's all *true* ..."

He drew in a deep breath, and Amelia braced herself. She wasn't sure for what – maybe James would scream. Or shout. Or get angry and attack Len. What she didn't expect was that he would sink back to the floor, roll himself into a ball and begin sobbing quietly.

"Are you serious?" Amelia hissed at him, kicking the sole of his shoe. "You finally wake up to reality and *this* is all you've got? You're the *worst*, James."

"So what now?" said Charlie. He was squatting in front of Len, looking at the alien with interest. "Do we just hang out here until Krskn comes to get us or what?"

The mention of the name was electric. A ferocious look of surprise flashed over Derek's face, and Len writhed in another explosive sneeze. A wave of mucus flew out of his mouth, smothering Charlie's whole lower body.

Charlie snorted at himself in amusement. "Oh, man! I'm saturated. Still," he nodded at Len respectfully, "cool defensive reaction. I wish I had one. Hey, Amelia – imagine Sophie T.'s face if I could do this. Oh – hey!" He slapped at his arms and legs. "This itches – it burns – ow! Hey, Len – ow! You're hard-core!"

Derek shook his head. "Get him out of here, Amelia. Take him somewhere he can towel it off his skin. *Don't* try to wash it, it'll only get worse."

"Got it," said Amelia.

Despite his cocky attitude, Charlie was beginning to look scared. "It really hurts, Amelia," he whispered.

She heard a sharp yelp outside the window. Was that Grawk? Derek looked startled, but only said, "Quickly, before he blisters."

Amelia couldn't think about anything else. She rushed Charlie from the room.

CHAPTER SIX

Bundling Charlie through the library and out to the lobby, Amelia ignored all the gasps of dismay, even Mary's. Her only thought was to get Charlie upstairs as quickly as she could and cover him in towels.

She'd forgotten to take a candle with her, but there was enough light from the candelabra on the reception desk for her to make out the twin staircases.

"Come on, Charlie," she urged. "We'll go up to the guest wing. It's not far."

He only whimpered in reply, but let her drag him on.

At the top of the stairs it was pitch-black, but the linen closet was at the end of the corridor, and it would be faster to do it blind than run back for a candle. Amelia ran her hand along the wall and counted the doorways, Charlie stumbling along behind her. Lightning flashed through the window at the far end, and Amelia sped up. Turning the bend after the last guest room, she felt the cupboard's handles and pulled.

Mary had already taken armloads of towels and blankets down to the Scouts, and at first Amelia felt only bare shelves. But climbing up on the bottom shelf, she reached the very top and pulled down a slab of folded material. She had no idea what it was, and didn't care. Roughly shaking it out, she wrapped Charlie from head to toe and started rubbing at him through the fabric.

After a minute or two he started to relax a bit, and then was able to help Amelia and finish off his own legs. Finally, he emerged from under the cloth and Amelia heard it fall to the ground.

"Are you OK?" she whispered.

"I wouldn't want that to happen to anyone," he said in a shaky voice. "I even wish I hadn't joked about Sophie T. ..."

They crept back along the corridor towards the lobby, Charlie carrying the cloth and occasionally rubbing at his skin and gasping. It seemed darker than ever now that Amelia didn't have an emergency to focus on. Down in the library, with so many people and candles together, she'd started to feel a bit safer from Krskn. Up here, alone with Charlie in the back of the hotel, the full sense of danger flooded back to her. Dad was a prisoner, Grawk had run off, and who knew where Mum was. James was a wreck, and Tom was in his cottage, and might as well have been separated from them by an ocean.

Amelia shivered and kept walking. They were about halfway along the corridor now, and the candles in the lobby below gave just enough light for Amelia to make out the railing around the gallery.

A shadow stepped out from the wall – a black shape so nearly invisible against the gloom that Amelia wasn't sure what she'd seen, only that it *moved*. Charlie sucked in a breath, and Amelia knew he'd seen it too.

"It's OK," said a low voice. "It's me."

"Lady Naomi?" said Charlie.

"Yes."

"Really?" said Amelia. "We can't see you. And even if we could, so what? A holo-emitter changes your voice, too, doesn't it?"

"True," said the shadow. "But a holo-emitter

wouldn't know we watched together as the Brin-Hask destroyed your kitchen in a battle against cyborg rats."

"Good point," said Charlie.

"A holo-emitter wouldn't know that," Amelia admitted. "But Krskn could have easily tortured the information out of the real Lady Naomi."

"True again," said the shadow, "although I'd like to think I wouldn't make it *easy* for Krskn, even under torture. Very well, Amelia – you choose a question for me. Something Krskn wouldn't have thought to get out of me."

Amelia thought hard.

"What's your secret research about?" Charlie said.

The shadow laughed. "Nice try, Charlie."

"Where was my brother the first time he saw you?" said Amelia.

"On the steps at the front entrance to the hotel,"

said the shadow. "He was wearing a Robotics Club sweatshirt from his old high school and humming to himself."

"Well ..." said Amelia. "I don't know about the humming, but yes, that's right." She felt awkward now. "Sorry. No offense."

"None taken," said Lady Naomi. "It was extremely wise to check. I have something for you, by the way."

Amelia stepped forward, straining her eyes in the dark. No matter how hard she tried, Lady Naomi was still just a vague shape, black on black. Amelia trailed her fingers along the wall to guide her and moved towards the gallery, Charlie beside her.

"This will be a shock," said Lady Naomi, "but I need you to keep quiet as you absorb it. I heard all the noise down there before, and it sounded like the guests are getting close to panic. Another scare, and they could go over the edge."

That didn't sound good to Amelia, but she swallowed hard and said, "OK."

"Here," said Lady Naomi, and she put a piece of string into Amelia's hand.

"What?" Amelia was confused. The string stood up vertically from her hand, but the end dangled softly. A soft glow bobbed above her head. She heard a muffled rumble and gasped, "Grawk?"

"What's going on?" said Charlie.

Lady Naomi tsk-ed impatiently. "Not enough light ... I forget ..." After a couple of seconds, a long flame wavered out of a lighter.

Amelia blinked in what seemed like bright light – then blinked again as she saw that the string in her hand was connected to a floating sphere the size of a beach ball. It was as delicate and wobbly-looking as a soap bubble, but inside was Grawk.

"What the –?" Charlie started.

Lady Naomi cut him off. "A containment field." She poked the bubble roughly. Instead of popping, or even floating away from her finger, the surface just flexed at the pressure and shimmered. "Totally impenetrable. Totally immovable." She pushed hard against the bubble with the palm of

her hand. "It only moves by that guiding rein." She nodded towards the string in Amelia's hand.

"But why did you put Grawk in there?" said Charlie.

"I didn't. I found him like that, just floating in midair over the lawn outside the library."

"Hang on," said Charlie. "Do you mean to say you can *see in the dark?*"

"A little bit," said Lady Naomi.

"Krskn," said Amelia, still staring at Grawk. "He did this, didn't he?"

Lady Naomi nodded. Who else would it have been? Amelia found it terrifying to learn that Krskn had *two* ways to trap people. First the binding tar, now these floating prisons. How many other weapons did he have to use against them? He might really be unstoppable.

Perhaps Lady Naomi saw all this in Amelia's face, because she said quickly, "It's not over yet,

Amelia. Whatever Krskn is up to, no one's been hurt yet, have they? In his own way, it looks like Krskn is taking good care of his targets. Whoever is behind this, they must be paying Krskn a premium to make sure all his captives are in perfect health."

Amelia couldn't answer, but nodded. She hoped Lady Naomi was right.

"On top of that," Lady Naomi said, "Tom told me the Lellum have got a Keeper on the way to protect them."

"Derek," said Charlie. "He's already here."

"Really?" Lady Naomi sounded startled. "Since when?"

"He arrived with the other guests," said Amelia. "They all piled in at once. I think at first no one could tell who was who, but it was obvious once Len got sick. Derek knew exactly what to do."

"Did he?" Lady Naomi's voice was stiff, wary.

"And what did he do? Exactly."

"He got us to take Len into the annex, and put water on him, and –"

"The *annex?*" said Lady Naomi. "Oh no –"

But then a scream of utter pain ripped through the hotel.

Amelia gasped. "James!"

CHAPTER SEVEN

Without a word, Lady Naomi gripped Amelia's hand and ran for the stairs.

"Hold on!" Charlie called after them. Without Lady Naomi's night vision to guide him, he was far slower, stumbling a couple of times on the stairs until the candlelight in the lobby gave him a chance to catch up.

Lady Naomi paused with Amelia by the library door. "You have to leave him here," she said, reaching for the string that controlled Grawk's containment field. Amelia hadn't even noticed she was still holding it, but now she pulled it away from Lady Naomi.

"No," she said fiercely. "I'm not losing him again. I'm not leaving behind any more of my family."

Charlie reached them, puffing slightly. His arms were swollen with welts from Len's toxic mucus.

"Here," he said, throwing the sheet he was carrying over the bubble. It should have been impossible for the frail-looking ball to support the weight, but it didn't budge. Now, when Amelia shortened the string so that Grawk floated only an inch above her hand, it just looked like she was carrying a bundle of laundry. Sort of.

"Fine," said Lady Naomi, and they pushed their way into the library.

Inside, Mary was frantic. Scout kids were running around in sheer panic, and the leaders weren't doing any better.

"Please!" Mary was shouting. "We all need to stay calm!"

At that moment, from behind the annex door, James let out another bloodcurdling scream of agony.

The Scouts screamed back and scrambled over one another, looking for a way to escape. The aliens seemed to have forgotten that what was outside was far worse than whatever was happening inside.

A sound of smashing glass came from inside the annex, and the Scouts lost all control. Even the humans, who had no idea of the true danger, got caught up in the panic. Maddened by fear, they were desperate to run – it didn't matter where. They swarmed around the library, shrieking and colliding with one another until someone threw open the French doors. With a great cry, they rushed into the hotel grounds.

"They've lost their minds!" said Mary. "What can we do?"

"Nothing for them," said Lady Naomi. "We've got to help James."

"But if Krskn's out there –"

Lady Naomi shook her head. "I don't think so."

They crossed the now-empty room and slid open the annex door. At first, Amelia thought it was empty, too. There was no Len, no Derek, and no glass in the big bay window. Then James howled again, and Amelia saw him hidden in the shadows, his whole body contorting with pain and ... glistening.

"Slime!" Charlie yelled, ripping the sheet off Grawk's bubble. "He's been slimed, same as me!" He threw the sheet over James and started rubbing. "It's all over his face and hands, too," Charlie continued frantically, his own face full of fear and pity.

Amelia dropped to her knees beside him and helped scrub the mucus off James.

When James at last stopped groaning and was able to sit up, Lady Naomi was deep in thought, looking at the slimy patch where Len had lain. Mary had fetched a clean, dry towel and now gave it to James.

"What happened?" said Lady Naomi.

James shook his head. "I don't know. I was just sitting here –"

Freaking out and crying, Amelia thought, but without any actual irritation now.

"– and Derek was talking to Len ..."

"Talking about what?" said Lady Naomi.

"At first he was just telling Len he'd get better soon, and everything would be OK, but when he saw I was listening, he bent over and whispered into Len's ... whatever ... and then Len exploded slime all over me."

James closed his eyes at the memory and shivered.

"And then?" Lady Naomi prompted.

"I couldn't see anything. The slime was all over my face, and then it started burning me, and I was screaming, but no one helped me, and then –" James opened his eyes and looked at Lady Naomi. "I heard glass smash, and lots of screaming, but I couldn't do anything. That's when you guys came. Thanks, by the way," he added to Charlie.

"So you didn't see what happened to Len or Derek?" Lady Naomi pressed.

"No. I was too busy thinking my eyeballs were on fire," said James.

"Did Krskn take them both?" Amelia asked.

"Both?" said Lady Naomi. "No, just Len."

"But what happened to Derek?" said Charlie. "Did Krskn vaporize him? Or has he gone after Krskn to get Len back?"

"Look –" Lady Naomi pointed to the smashed window. "Where's the glass? If Krskn smashed in from outside, there should be broken glass all over the floor right where Len was lying. But –"

"Nothing," said Amelia. "Where did the glass go?"

"It's all over the veranda outside."

"You think Derek smashed through the window to escape Krskn?" said Charlie. "Or are you saying he let Krskn in?"

"I'm saying Derek *is* Krskn," said Lady Naomi.

"But Derek is the Keeper!" said Charlie.

"How do you know that?"

"Because he said so!" Charlie shot back, then realized how weak that argument was. "Oh."

"It was Derek who gave Len the salty cookie!" said Amelia, suddenly realizing. "He handed it to Len himself. He made him sick on purpose!"

"Sounds like the perfect test to see who was

Lellum and who was human." Lady Naomi's expression darkened. "And the perfect excuse to separate Len from the group and get him into the annex."

"... where he could smash *out* through the window and drag him away," Charlie finished.

Lady Naomi nodded. "Yes, that's exactly what Krskn wants us to believe. But that's not what happened here. The smashed window was just a distraction – an attempt to put us off his real escape route."

"What escape route?" said Charlie. "Through the library, you mean?"

"No." Mary was certain. "That door didn't open."

"Then where did he go?" said Charlie.

Amelia looked up at the ceiling. Just in case Len had crawled up there, or was floating in a bubble like Grawk's. For all she knew, Krskn could fly.

But nothing was there.

Lady Naomi sighed. "He was very clever to bring Len here, but what I don't understand is how he could have known about it. Unless ..."

She paused and then put her hand to her forehead. "The rats!"

"What?" said Charlie.

"The cybernetically enhanced rats the Brin-Hask destroyed," she said.

Amelia's stomach swooped. "The rats were being used by someone else. They were spying on the whole hotel. Passing on our secrets –"

"Yes," said Lady Naomi. "And now it looks as though they were passing them on to Krskn. Or at least, someone who was selling information to Krskn."

"What information?" said Amelia. "Where do you think Krskn went?"

"And when are we going to stop *talking* about it,

and go and rescue Len?" said Charlie.

Lady Naomi looked grim, hesitated, and then crossed to the very place James was standing. Swollen and lumpy as he was with mucus burns, he still blushed as he moved out of her way. She reached up to a little framed picture of fish swimming through coral, and tilted it to sit at an angle.

Without a sound, a trapdoor fell open in the opposite corner of the room, leaving an ominous black hole in the floor. Lady Naomi carried the candle over to it and, following her, Amelia saw two rough wooden steps inside the floor cavity. A dank stone staircase had been cut directly into the rock of the headland beneath them, the same headland that was riddled with natural caves and tunnels.

"How did you know about that?" Charlie blurted out.

"I've been here a long time," said Lady Naomi quietly.

After ten or fifteen more seconds, the trapdoor silently closed again, and turning to look behind her, Amelia saw the picture had straightened itself on the wall.

What kind of place *was* this?

"So what do we do?" she said.

"You do nothing," said Lady Naomi.

"But what about Len?" Charlie protested.

"*You* do nothing," said Lady Naomi. "*I* will go and track Krskn down. If he's already gotten away with kidnapping Len, then unfortunately there is nothing any of us can do. But I'm betting Krskn will be unwilling to leave with just one Lellum. I think he's probably still on the hunt. Which is dangerous for all of us, but offers a slim chance for Len. It gives me a tiny window to try to rescue him."

"Well, if nowhere is safe," said Charlie, "I might as well come with you."

"And me," said Amelia.

"No, Charlie!" said his mum. "You're going to stay right here! You promised me – you both did – that you wouldn't leave the hotel again."

"And we won't," said Charlie. "We won't even leave this room, if you think about it."

"Don't play the lawyer with me, Karolos Floros!" Mary's voice was shrill. "This isn't a game."

"I'm not," he said gently. "But you know I'm right. If we sit here and do nothing to help Len, we're in exactly the same amount of danger. And if we're going to get kidnapped anyway, I'd rather at least be trying to stop Krskn, not just giving up and hoping he doesn't notice us."

Mary stared at him, speechless, but then her expression softened to one of reluctant pride.

"I haven't said you can come with me," said Lady Naomi.

But Amelia knew Charlie had won. They'd be

safer with Lady Naomi than with his mum, and both the adults knew it.

"What about me?" said James shakily. "What do I do? Am I going with you, too?"

Lady Naomi frowned at him, and Amelia knew what she saw: a wreck. It wasn't just the red welts left by the burns, or the way James's eyes had swollen to painful slits, still streaming tears. No, the real problem was that James had simply been through too much tonight. He was trying to accept reality, but he'd avoided so much of it for so long, it was too big for him to take in one go. He looked about ten seconds away from a total nervous breakdown.

"I need you to stay here," said Lady Naomi kindly. "You and Mary have to keep the hotel secure and be ready to bring the Scouts back inside whenever they get over their panic. Will you do that for me?"

James nodded.

"Right." Lady Naomi tipped the picture on the wall to the side once more. "Stay close behind me, you two. And no more talking once we get into the tunnel, OK?"

Charlie put a finger to his lips, Amelia picked up the string of Grawk's containment field, and one by one, they followed Lady Naomi into the darkness beyond the trapdoor.

CHAPTER EIGHT

It's all very well for Lady Naomi, thought Amelia. *Anyone could be silent and stealthy if they could see in the dark.*

For Amelia and Charlie, though, following Lady Naomi meant feeling their way inch by inch, hands tracing the rough stone walls, feet probing the empty air in front of them for the next step down into the caves. Grawk's luminous eyes gave off enough light for Amelia to see the texture of the walls beside her, but not enough to show the steps below.

It was slow, frustrating work, with nothing to hear but her own footsteps, Charlie's just ahead of her, and the occasional hiss from him when he accidentally bumped one of his welts. From Lady Naomi there came no sound at all. She might as well have been a ghost. Or not there at all. They could be walking into the center of the Earth all on their own ...

At last the floor leveled out, and there were no more steps to navigate. Amelia felt something touch her and pulled away, but Charlie murmured, "It's me. Here, take my hand."

He pulled her forward, and Amelia realized Lady Naomi must be leading him along.

The narrow stairwell had widened into a cavern broad enough that Amelia could no longer touch the walls beside her. The ground was hard and flat under their feet – like tiles or floorboards – and every now and then, when Grawk's head turned in the right direction, Amelia thought she could make out shapes in the darkness – the shadowy outline of a counter or a glint of light reflecting off glass.

"It's some kind of laboratory," breathed Charlie.

Lady Naomi said nothing.

"It is, isn't it?" Charlie pressed. "This is where you do your research!"

"*Shh,*" said Lady Naomi. Then, "No, but if you can't be silent, go back *now*."

She was quiet, but so fierce that Charlie didn't dare speak again.

They kept walking and soon the floor gave way to rough, sandy ground. Somewhere in the distance, Amelia could hear waves crashing. Lady Naomi led them along a winding path, deeper and deeper into ... wherever this was. Sometimes there was a drop in temperature for a second, or a louder sound of the sea in the distance, and she guessed there were tunnels branching off in different directions along the way. Without a flashlight or a map or even a ball of string to guide them back, Amelia knew they'd be completely lost without Lady Naomi.

She gulped and reminded herself that they'd already proven Lady Naomi was Lady Naomi, and not Krskn with a holo-emitter.

Amelia blinked, peering again into the dark. Was she imagining things, or could she see slightly? Maybe a whole night without light was making her brain play tricks on her – or maybe she was just seeing spots from the glow of Grawk's eyes ... but no, she could definitely make out the faint gray line of Charlie's head in front of her. She gazed at the walls. She could *see* them. The caves were *glowing* now. Blue and yellow lichens on the rocks were emitting a pale light.

As they walked, the lichens grew thicker and

the light strengthened until Amelia could easily see the ground ahead. She and Charlie dropped hands. They passed into a little grotto where the lichens were especially bright, with feathery pink fronds. It was so beautiful, and somehow knowing they weren't allowed to speak made it seem almost magical.

Amelia could see now where the tunnels split off. Often Lady Naomi had to choose between two or three forks in their path, but she seemed to know exactly what she was doing.

They had walked so far that Amelia wondered which part of the headland they could be under now. Had they gone as far as the hedge maze? As the old magnolias? As Lady Naomi led them around a corner, Amelia saw a carved archway, and beyond it a vast chamber, like a cathedral, bigger than the concourse at the airport. It was set with glass along the walls, and two rows of huge pillars, thicker than palm tree trunks, holding up the roof.

Stepping through the archway, Amelia noticed a heavy metal door raised up like a guillotine blade and ready to drop closed behind them. An identical door was open in an archway at the opposite end of the chamber, and beyond that, a pitch-black space that she guessed was another tunnel. The sandy ground had given way to a stone floor, not solid, but cut into complicated patterns. It was like one enormous storm water drain cover, but done as beautifully as a Persian carpet. Overhead, the raw rock had been carved into a handsome vaulted ceiling, archways crisscrossing each other as they spanned the distances between the pillars. Lichen alone couldn't have lit such a massive space. Behind the glass walls, Amelia saw dozens of glowing glass spheres.

She started in surprise. Those weren't glass

walls – they were doors. Dozens and dozens of different sized glass doors, each one covering an empty, carved space behind. They were *rooms*.

Amelia looked around in amazement. It was dry and empty now, but if you filled all this with water, it would look exactly like the lobby and guest wings of a hotel designed for *fish*. In fact, looking more closely, she could see metal tubing and blocks of pumice in each room, like giant versions of the air stones in the aquarium at school.

Lady Naomi stopped walking and drummed her fingers against her thigh. She padded from one glass room to the next, peering inside. Amelia followed behind, still dragging Grawk in his containment field, and Charlie by her side. So they were all together when Lady Naomi found Len trapped inside a pulsating bubble behind one of the pillars.

He was hunched into a ball, his antennae

retracted, and the space inside the bubble was gradually filling up with foaming green mucus as he tried desperately to protect himself.

When Lady Naomi spoke, her voice jarred after so much silence. "It's a trap, isn't it?"

There was no noise anywhere. No movement. No sign or clue to suggest why Lady Naomi would say such a thing.

Amelia looked around the chamber wildly. Nothing! But Len was still bubbling away with that vicious, frightened slime ...

"What –?" Charlie started.

"Run," said Lady Naomi very quietly.

Before Amelia could even register the word, a jet of black tar hit Lady Naomi in the face and knocked her backward. As she hit the ground, there was another flash of movement – but so fast, Amelia couldn't tell from what direction – and Lady Naomi began slowly drifting upward, her entire body enclosed in a transparent containment sphere, just like Grawk's and Len's.

Charlie darted forward to grab the guiding string dangling from the bottom of the bubble. Half a second later, he was floating helplessly next to Lady Naomi in a bubble of his own. He screamed in rage, but Amelia heard only the faintest muffled noise.

Amelia stood frozen, her mind blank with terror, as Grawk leapt inside his bubble. Amelia could hear only the dim echo of his bark. He glared at something behind her, his ears flat against his head. On pure instinct, she dived in the opposite direction, finding cover behind one of the great stone pillars.

Panting, she looked back. The place she had been the instant before was now occupied by a huge, empty bubble.

What do I do? she screamed silently.

She couldn't see Lady Naomi or Charlie from here, not without sticking her head out from behind the pillar. Looking one way, she could see the very edge of Len's containment field. The other way, nothing. She looked up.

Her heart almost stopped beating. Tucked behind one of the sloping arches in the ceiling was another containment field. It bobbed like a balloon, and inside was –

Mum. Amelia wanted to cry, but pinched herself hard on the leg instead. *Think!*

She scanned the rest of the ceiling. It was a mass of shadows and hiding places, each archway in the vault creating another deep hollow. Each one, for all she knew, housed another containment field, keeping another person prisoner. Maybe her dad was up there by now ...

Then, like something oily and impossible from a nightmare, she saw a body slip out of the

shadows and slither weightlessly across the ceiling. Long black legs swiveled in their hips at angles that should have dislocated them. A tail moved sinuously in time with a long neck. A narrow head kept its eyes fixed continuously on Amelia.

Krskn, Amelia thought.

He seemed to *flow* towards her, as though gravity couldn't touch him. She watched him walk lazily down a pillar, the claws of his back legs gripping to the stone, his body upright as though standing on the flat ground. He reached the floor, and walked over to Amelia without so much as blinking.

She stared at his lizard-like body. The black rippling skin wasn't scaly, but matte like velvet, and very soft looking. *Like a salamander.* His eyes were deep red, wide open, and snake-ish. From nose to tail, he was long and elegant, but he had broad shoulders, a deep chest, and both his hands and feet were clawed. He opened his mouth and a tongue flickered out between sharp, white teeth.

He's gorgeous, Amelia thought. Terrifying, vicious and evil, obviously, but who knew he would also be so ... magnificent?

Krskn looked down at her cringing at the foot of the pillar, and sneered, "So good of you to come to me, Amelia. All of you! I was almost ready to leave with just the human female and this one repulsive Lellum." He touched a button on the back of his wrist cuff, and all the containment fields wafted gently down to float in a line between him and Amelia. Even Grawk's string pulled out of her hand and obediently drifted over to Krskn. Five shimmering bubbles in a row.

Krskn smirked, took a small silver tube from his belt and toyed with it as he spoke. "Now look at all my prizes! The Lellum specimen I was contracted to acquire, but also an infant grawk –

honestly, I'm doing you a favor taking him off your hands, I really am. You have no idea what you'd be dealing with when he's full grown – "

He walked along the row and peered at Charlie and Mum. "Two humans – the small one might be sold as a pet once I remove his tongue; the adult, though ... is this your mother, Amelia? I thought so. She's very clever, isn't she? She caught me going down one of the other access tunnels and followed me nearly the whole way here before I realized. Marvelous. In fact, a pity she wasn't armed to deal with my containment gun – I might have actually had a decent fight on my hands." He sighed and smiled at Amelia. "Oh, don't worry – I would have *won* ..."

Amelia shifted into a crouch. When Krskn's blow finally landed, she wanted to be ready. She half wished he'd hurry up and end it, but he was having too much fun gloating.

"And you ..." Krskn reached Lady Naomi's bubble and tapped it curiously. "What might you be, my dear?"

Lady Naomi refused to look at him. The tar covered her mouth and one eye, but she didn't try to shift it. She balanced on the curved floor of her containment field with perfect composure and gazed at Amelia.

Krskn flipped the silver tube in his hand and laughed. "Do you know, I was almost going to let you go, Amelia. Leave you here to wonder for the rest of your life what I did with your family. But," he grinned charmingly, "then I remembered I'd left good old Dad in the shed! He looks the type whose heart would break over losing all of you, doesn't he? So ..." He leaned down, stretched out his neck, put his mouth to Amelia's ear and murmured, "I'm going to trap you and sell you as the pathetic, hairless Earth monkey you really are."

She felt hypnotized. Even though he was threatening her and her family in the cruelest and most offensive way he could, the closer he got to her, the more dazed and helpless she felt. Once, she had been made dizzy with joy by some intoxicating alien eggs; this was like that, only worse. There was no pleasure in being mesmerized by Krskn, only the ghastly sense of being frozen to the spot. He was pointing that silver tube at her, and as soon as he fired, it would all be over, and there was nothing she could do. She closed her eyes and waited for the end.

From somewhere, a vaguely familiar voice said, "That's enough, Krskn."

CHAPTER NINE

Krskn kept the containment tube pointed at Amelia, but his head whipped around to glare towards the far end of the chamber, where the doorway opened onto an unlit tunnel.

Amelia's mind raced. Was it possible that these tunnels led all the way out to the gateway itself? That would make sense – an aquatic alien visitor could hardly come up Tom's staircase and walk overland to the hotel. But whenever the gateway opened, there was always sound or a smell or a gust of air or a flash of light or *something* – and Amelia had neither heard nor felt anything to signal the arrival of a new connection. If the gateway were there, it must be closed.

And yet, out of the darkness stepped a tall, thin, frail-looking figure in a long black coat.

"Leaf Man," Amelia gasped.

Krskn glanced her way, and snorted with contempt. "*Leaf Man*, is it now? How delightful. Well, come on in, sir. Join our little party."

Amelia was baffled. The last time she'd seen Leaf Man, he was walking away from the total annihilation of the cyber-rats in their kitchen. *Someone* had set off a self-destruct program that blew up their central control system, and no one had ever found out who that someone was.

Tom trusted Leaf Man, but Amelia had serious doubts. Perhaps Leaf Man had merely been watching the Brin-Hask battle, the same as Amelia, Charlie and Lady Naomi. Perhaps he had killed the rats to help Amelia's parents avoid trouble with Gateway Control. Or perhaps Leaf Man had been the one to engineer the rats in the first place. Perhaps he was the spy – the very person who had sold Krskn the information about the trapdoor in the annex. For all Amelia knew, Leaf Man was the one who had contracted Krskn to come here and steal Lellum kids.

She looked over at Lady Naomi, wishing she could tell Amelia what to believe.

Amelia thought harder. She remembered the first time she and Charlie had met Leaf Man – he'd told her he was "nobody from nowhere." At the time, she'd thought it was a kind of annoying modesty, or a joke, but what if it had been the truth? What had Tom said about the dangers of the gateway? That if you got sucked into the space *between* wormholes, you'd be lost forever in the Nowhere.

She stared at Leaf Man. If he came from the Nowhere, if it were his natural home, then he could probably come and go through the gateway without using wormholes at all. In fact, that's probably what he'd just done right now, slipping out of the void without a sound. And if he could do that, then perhaps that made him ...

"The Keeper!" Amelia said loudly.

Krskn snarled in disgust, and faster than Amelia could follow, he flicked the containment tube away from Amelia and shot at Leaf Man.

Leaf Man sprang up, leaping half the length of the chamber, and landed lightly in front of Krskn. "I want the prisoners released."

Krskn spat. "And I want to leave here with seven of you for the Guild – imagine how much I'll get when I add a human girl and a failed Keeper to my auction list."

He pounced at Leaf Man, but Leaf Man

jumped again, this time straight up. He sailed up into the shadows of the ceiling and must have clung there, because he didn't come down again. Amelia peered up after him, but saw nothing. Krskn ran up the nearest pillar and sped across the underside of the vault in pursuit.

For a second Amelia was too shocked to move, but then she gathered up all five strings and dragged the containment bubbles over to the tunnel leading to the hotel. She'd just made it to the archway when a flurry of noise and movement behind made her turn. She saw a tangle of black and white fall to the ground. Krskn and Leaf Man landed with a thud on the stone floor, a small silver object rolling away from them.

Without thinking, Amelia sprinted forward and grabbed it. Krskn's containment tube! Had luck finally begun to turn her way? Straightening up, she had her answer.

No.

Where Krskn and Leaf Man had fallen from the roof, where she might have hoped to see Krskn knocked out cold, if not dead from the impact, she saw instead two identical figures pick themselves up, brush themselves off, and look at her with identical expressions on their narrow white faces.

"Two Leaf Men," she murmured.

"No," said the Leaf Man on her right. "Only one of us is a Keeper. The other is Krskn – the one who has imprisoned your entire family."

"You keep forgetting about James!" Amelia snapped. She wasn't sure why that was the point that made her lose her temper, but now she had the weapon, she wasn't going to be pushed around anymore.

If only she knew how to undo the containment fields, she could get Len to blast them both with mucus and break their holo-emitters. It would be unfair on the real Leaf Man to get burned, but at least it would be proof.

Seeing as she couldn't do that ... "I'm going to shoot you both. Then I can get Tom, and let him work out who's who."

The Leaf Man on the left shook his head. "You wouldn't have time. If you shot me first, Krskn there would attack you before you could do so much as blink."

"Very convincing!" said the Leaf Man on the right. "You sound so sincere – yes, you're just trying to help, aren't you? Getting the girl to shoot *me* first when we both know that *you're* Krskn!"

The Leaf Man on the left shrugged. "She will make her own decision. I trust she can see past these holo-emitter disguises. If she's half as smart as her mother, she already suspects which one of us is Krskn."

Do I? I have a feeling, but can I trust it?

The Leaf Man on the right smiled at her. "Amelia," he said kindly.

But Amelia had seen that smile before. On Derek's handsome face as he passed the salted cookie to Len. In Krskn's splendid eyes as he'd promised to kidnap her. She knew exactly what lay behind that warmth and charm.

"Hello, Krskn," she said, pointing the containment tube at him. *Now if only I knew how to fire it.*

"Amelia!" He stepped back, raising his hands in surrender, his black Leaf Man eyes unblinking and expressionless. "Don't waste your shot! I'm the Keeper!"

Amelia ignored him and raised the tube, still pointing at him, until she could see it without taking her eyes off him. Was there a button somewhere?

"It responds to pressure," said the Leaf Man

on the left. He turned his head a fraction to the side, almost like he was listening for something. "When you've decided on your target, just squeeze it hard and the containment field will deploy."

When I decide on my target? she puzzled. *Haven't I already decided? I know which one's Krskn – what's to decide?*

Leaf Man on the right saw her confusion and seized his opportunity. "You see? He's let slip the truth by accident! He knows you should shoot him, not me!"

Amelia, knowing she was risking everything, looked away from Leaf Man on the right and looked long and hard at Leaf Man on the left instead.

"That's right!" said Leaf Man on the right. "Shoot him – save yourself!"

I don't want to save myself, thought Amelia. *I want to save everyone. The Keeper would understand that.* She hesitated, not knowing where to point the tube.

Leaf Man on the left nodded, and said quietly, "He's a liar, you know. Cruel, selfish, greedy and a shameless liar. But he's right about one thing: you *should* shoot me."

What?

Was this some sort of weird double bluff? Or did he really mean it? If he *was* the Keeper, then for some reason she couldn't see, he was asking Amelia to shoot him. And if he *wasn't* the Keeper... Well, she'd be happy to shoot Krskn.

Amelia knew that if she got this wrong, they would all be prisoners or slaves, or worse, on the other side of the galaxy by this time tomorrow.

She wavered, unable to untangle what should happen next.

Leaf Man on the left's head turned to the side again – and again, it was almost as if he could hear something Amelia couldn't. His tone was urgent, but his blank white face gave nothing away. "You need to choose now. Please. Shoot me."

She did.

As soon as she squeezed the tube, she knew she'd gotten it wrong. She wanted to take back her decision even as the blast of white gel shot out towards the Leaf Man on the left. Before she had time to blink, a huge transparent bubble had engulfed his whole body.

Her hand shook, still nervously holding the silver tube.

From her right, a fluid black shape swarmed over her. A tail curled around her legs and pulled against them, spinning her around violently. For a moment she was dizzy and confused, and the next thing she knew she was alone on the stone floor and the tube was gone.

"Brilliant work, Amelia my love!" said Krskn. "Masterful!"

She looked up and watched as he shot her point-blank.

The containment field thumped into her, and she fell back, waiting for the pain as she hit the ground with her head. Instead, there was only a warm, rolling sensation of being inside the bubble – as if she'd fallen inside a bounce house. She was trapped like the rest of them. There they were – Krskn's seven captives, like ships in bottles. She wanted to be sick, but she knew she'd only have to stand in it, like poor Len in his froth.

Krskn danced on the chamber floor, gloating over his victory.

"Oh, *Amelia*," Krskn sang, his voice melodious, but so hateful and greasy too. And Amelia could hear every word. Although the bubbles muffled any sound made inside, Krskn's taunting outside was coming through loud and clear.

"What a perfect, pitiful little fool you are – and I'm so grateful to you! The great Keeper of the Gates and Ways neutralized by an idiot child. It's so delicious, Amelia, I'm going to make you a promise. Really! I promise," he laid a claw over his muscular chest, "that when we get to Absin Delta, I'll make sure I sell you to someone who wants a pet, and not pet *food!*"

He laughed heartily and turned to Leaf Man. "You disgraceful invertebrate! You sniveling waste of carbon! If I had even half your powers, do you think I'd –"

But Leaf Man wasn't listening. At least, he wasn't listening to Krskn. But Amelia saw he *was* concentrating on something. Then she heard it, too – a deep, gargling roll of thunder, like being caught under a giant wave in the surf, like –

Leaf Man nodded quietly, and the huge metal door Amelia, Charlie and Lady Naomi had earlier walked through dropped closed, sealing them all in with Krskn. That thundering sound deepened, and then –

Water blasted into the chamber from all directions – seawater crashing up through the slatted rock floor, and a black torrent rushing down the tunnel from the gateway. It was *open*.

Amelia panicked, and saw Charlie and Len thrashing in their bubbles too. Grawk was barking, and when the waters hit, Krskn was thrown to the ground by the sheer force of the onslaught. The water level was rising so quickly, it would be over their heads in less than a second.

She took in a huge gulp of air, then another, petrified, helpless. Would the bubble hold her underwater while she drowned? And then she looked again at Len's slime – none of that had leaked out. The containment fields were waterproof. Although the sound could get in, the water was kept out. Better yet, without anyone operating the guiding strings, the bubbles were all fixed in place. Even as Krskn was being dashed against a pillar by the water's momentum, the seven prisoners were totally safe. It was like being in their own tiny underwater observatories.

Amelia watched as Krskn recovered from his collision. The water had completely filled the chamber now, so the currents were lessening.

A crocodile can hold its breath for fifteen minutes. It can stay underwater for up to two hours, if it's not stressed – how long can Krskn survive before he drowns?

She looked around for the containment tube. *He has salamander skin – hopefully the salt water will burn him up, same as it would Len ...*

But Krskn showed no signs of distress. His long tail drove him through the water like an eel, and he was swimming straight for *her* – his claws stretched out, his mouth split into a grin, and those red eyes locked on to the guiding string dangling beneath her feet. He turned his head, and she saw that gills had opened along his neck.

He doesn't even need to hold his breath! He's probably more dangerous underwater than he was on dry land! And it's me he's angry at.

But as Krskn reached for the string, the entire chamber was hit by a shock wave, and he faltered. In that split second, Amelia realized the tremor must have come from the gateway. It was still open. And there was nothing between this chamber and the gateway itself.

Amelia remembered the fear in Tom's face when he'd had to walk down the stairs to the gateway the day that Grawk had arrived. And that was after the wormhole had passed and the gateway had closed. He'd told them that the gateway was *never* safe, that *anything* could come through, that they could be sucked into the Nowhere and lost forever.

And if she'd had any doubt that Tom was telling the truth, the flash of alarm in Krskn's eyes convinced her otherwise.

He lashed his tail again, reaching for the string of Amelia's bubble. It was almost in his hand when a deep, juddering noise boomed through the waters, and a flurry of bubbles rushed out from the gateway tunnel. Instead of grabbing the string, Krskn turned his head to look. It was that hesitation which saved Amelia, because the same moment, all the water was sucked back out of the cavern.

It was unimaginably violent. Even faster than the chamber had flooded, the water was torn away – and by a force far greater than Earth's gravity or the caves' intense magnetism. This was the vacuum of space itself, or not space – the terrible wrenching power unleashed when space was twisted open.

Krskn was nothing to this power. Amelia saw one last glimpse of his beautiful red eyes wide with horror before he was dragged away by the current and vanished through the gateway.

CHAPTER TEN

It was James and Tom who got them all out of the containment fields. They couldn't find Krskn's silver containment tube; it had probably been sucked through the gateway with him. And without that, Tom couldn't just reverse the fields and set them free instantly. Instead, he had a long consultation with Control while James paced around the empty chamber, wordlessly examining the glassed rooms, the glowing spheres, the size of the vaulted ceiling above them. Every now and then he just shook his head.

When Tom got back, he was carrying a big bottle of white vinegar and a bag of salt.

"We have to erode the fields manually," Amelia heard him say.

"Huh?" James stopped studying the carvings on the pillar closest to Amelia, and turned.

Tom handed him an old rag. "You add vinegar, sprinkle on salt, and scrub until the membrane wears away."

Len frothed and foamed anew in his field. Understandably, he was very unhappy about the prospect of being saved with salt and vinegar. James, on the other hand, was equally wary about bursting a bubble filled with toxic green mucus, so in the end Tom had to work on Len, while James started on Amelia.

It was the nicest time she'd spent with her brother in ages. She sat cross-legged on the floor of her prison, unable to talk back, while James, still sore and swollen from the burns, chatted away to her as he rubbed salt into the bubble. She could tell he was embarrassed by what had happened that night. It took him ages to meet her eyes, but it didn't matter. He was working hard to cheer her up. He was taking care of his little sister, just like he would have done a year ago, before things went so wrong with him.

When he had finally worn a hole big enough for Amelia to crawl through, she hugged him tightly.

"It's so good to see you, James," she said, and she knew he understood what she meant.

Then Tom limped past, handed her a rag, and told her to get to work on Charlie's bubble.

One by one, everyone was set free – except for Dad, who was still stuck to the wall of the shed above ground. And Lady Naomi, who still had tar over her face …

"Kerosene and butter," said Tom, patting Lady

Naomi on the shoulder. "Although apparently it will take a couple of hours to dissolve."

"I can't believe we won!" Charlie shrieked. "I can't believe Leaf Man was the hero! I can't believe I'm *alive!*"

Charlie was so happy, he even romped around with Grawk. They raced each other from one end of the chamber to the other, weaving in and out of the pillars, Charlie whooping with joy. Amelia laughed, but rather than joining in, she looked around for Leaf Man.

He'd disappeared.

"We didn't even say thank you!" said Amelia.

Tom didn't want to talk about it. "If he wanted to hang out and group hug with you all, he'd still be here, wouldn't he?"

Mum kissed the top of Amelia's head. "You'll see him again."

Amelia yawned and leaned into Mum. As the

adrenaline faded away, she realized how exhausted she was. And how cold. She felt as though she could sleep for a week. No, scratch that – she felt as though she could eat an entire chocolate cake and then sleep for a week. Her stomach gurgled. Yeah, she was starving.

But it wasn't over yet: they still had to walk back along all those long, dark tunnels and up those stairs to get to the hotel. After everything they'd been through, they weren't even home yet.

To Amelia's surprise, the walk home turned out to be fun. It was a much shorter journey when they were heading back to safety rather than down into danger, and when they could talk and laugh together. Mum hadn't seen glowing lichens in the tunnel she'd followed Krskn along, and she was as delighted as Amelia by the pink grotto.

James walked more slowly at the back of the group, keeping Len company as he inched along. The sandy ground was extremely hard work for his soft slug belly, especially as he'd already used up a lot of his slime, but James encouraged him with descriptions of all the lettuce and baby spinach they would give him in the hotel.

Amelia looked over her shoulder at the two of them, and nudged Mum.

Mum smiled. "I knew he'd get it in the end. It took longer than Dad and I thought, but he got there!"

It also took Tom longer than he thought to free Dad from the binding tar in the meter shed. The sun was up and already getting hot before Tom finally limped back to the hotel with Dad half draped over his shoulders. He was trying to walk by himself, but a whole night standing upright and immobile had left his legs rather wobbly. The tar still clung in chunks to his clothes, and he was white with fatigue, but he grinned when he saw Amelia running over the grass towards him.

"Cookie!"

She wrapped her arms around him, at last giving him the hug she'd missed out on the night before.

"Tom has been telling me how amazing you were. You and Charlie. Even James!"

Amelia looked sideways at Tom. She had her doubts that he'd said any such thing.

Tom just grunted. "Can you make your own way back to the hotel from here? I've got things to do." And without waiting for an answer, he shrugged off Dad's arm and turned to stump off down the hill again.

Dad staggered a bit and Amelia rushed to put her arms around him. He just laughed. "Good old Tom. He was impressed, you know. And even if he didn't say it quite like that, I'm saying it now.

You were a star last night, kiddo."

The praise was warm and genuine, but Amelia didn't feel like a star. What had happened last night was far too complicated for that. What she did feel, though, was happy. Truly and simply happy.

A flock of cockatoos flew across the blue sky, screeching outrageously. Far below them, the surf pounded against the foot of the headland. And in between, standing on the grass in the sunshine, was her whole family: Dad with his arm around her, Mum and James talking intensely together by the rose garden, and Charlie squirming to get away as his mum smothered him in yet another weeping bear hug.

"Mum!"

Mary crooned over him in Greek, but Charlie had had enough.

"I know! You've said it a million times!"

He struggled out of her arms. "But if you really loved me, you'd stop hugging me and get me some *toast!*"

Amelia laughed. "And me! I could eat a whole loaf!"

"Two loaves!" James threw in. "And then I'm going to bed until July."

"Actually," Mary said, "you might have forgotten – we still have fifty guests in the hotel."

Amelia sighed. It was true. While they'd been down in the caves struggling with Krskn, Mary had been sitting up in the library waiting for each hysterical Scout to calm down enough to make their way back to shelter. Human and Lellum alike, they'd all eventually crept back and were now spread out on the floor of the library, sleeping off the terror of the night before.

"What are we going to say when they wake up?" Amelia asked.

"I doubt we'll have to say anything," said Mum. "The Lellum know exactly what was going on last night, and once they see Len is safe, they'll save all their questions for the Keeper when he comes back to escort them through the gateway."

"But what about the humans?"

Mum raised an eyebrow and smiled. "What did they really see? A boy with an allergic reaction, a smashed window – nothing so very peculiar. In fact, the only really strange part about last night was how they all behaved, but even that will probably make sense to them – once they find out they spent the night in Australia's most haunted hotel."

Amelia laughed. "That's so mean! You're going to let them think the broken window and the screams were because of ghosts?"

"Are you kidding?" Mum laughed back. "This will be the stuff of Scouting legend! They'll tell this story at every campfire for the rest of their lives! And for once, it'll be a true story – more or less."

They made their way wearily up to the hotel steps. Then Amelia's dad spied the library annex window.

"Oh, no!" he groaned. "Not more broken glass – we just replaced every window in the kitchen."

Amelia laughed out loud. What a brilliant day when a broken window was all they had to worry about. Grawk bumped against her leg, and together they all went into the hotel. Home.

Cerberus Jones

Cerberus Jones is the three-headed writing team made up of Chris Morphew, Rowan McAuley and David Harding.

Chris Morphew is *The Gateway's* story architect. Chris's experience writing adventures for *Zac Power* and heart-stopping twists for *The Phoenix Files* makes him the perfect man for the job!

Rowan McAuley is the team's chief writer. Before joining Cerberus Jones, Rowan wrote some of the most memorable stories and characters in the best-selling *Go Girl!* series.

David Harding's job is editing and continuity. He is also the man behind *Robert Irwin's Dinosaur Hunter* series, as well as several *RSPCA Animal Tales* titles.

THE FOUR-FINGERED MAN

Cerberus Jones

THE WARRIORS OF BRIN-HASK

Cerberus Jones

FOUR GREAT ADVENTURES

THE MIDNIGHT MERCENARY

Cerberus Jones

THE ANCIENT STARSHIP

Cerberus Jones